Mickey's Young Readers Library

This Book Belongs to:

Mickey's
Young Readers Library

VOLUME

3

Minnie's Giant Plan

STORY BY DIANE NAMM

Activities by Thoburn Educational Enterprises, Inc.

A BANTAM BOOK
NEW YORK · TORONTO · LONDON · SYDNEY · AUCKLAND

Minnie's Giant Plan   A Bantam Book/September 1990. All rights reserved. © 1990 The Walt Disney Company. Developed by
The Walt Disney Company in conjunction with Nancy Hall, Inc. This book may not be reproduced or transmitted in any form or by any means.
ISBN 0–553–05616–6
Published simultaneously in the United States and Canada. Bantam Books are published by Bantam Doubleday Dell Publishing Group,
Inc. Its trademark, consisting of the words "Bantam Books" and the portrayal of a rooster, is Registered in U.S. Patent
and Trademark Office and in other countries. Marca Registrada. Bantam Books 666 Fifth Avenue, New York, New York 10103.
Printed in the United States of America
0 9 8 7 6 5 4 3 2
A Walt Disney BOOK FOR YOUNG READERS

One day, Elmo the friendly neighborhood giant rushed over to Minnie's house.

"Oh, Minnie—oh my! What are we going to do?" cried the giant.

"What's wrong?" Minnie asked.

"A terrible thing has happened," the giant began in a trembling voice. "A very mean, big giant—bigger than any giant you've ever seen—wants to fight with me! And if I don't win, he will make everyone, including ME, his prisoner!" Elmo finished, with a terrible sob.

"I see," said Minnie, slowly nodding her head.
"What are we to do? Where can we hide?"
Elmo cried. "I can't fight this enormous giant—I don't
even know how to fight!"

"Well, let's not hear another word about hiding," replied Minnie. "There isn't anywhere at all in a town as small as this that a giant as big as you and everyone else could hide." Then she thought for a moment. "Just how much time do we have before this mean giant gets here?" she asked.

As if in answer to her question, they heard a low rumble in the distance.

"Not too much time," Elmo wailed. "It sounds as if he is coming this way right now!"

"Stop that crying, this minute!" Minnie told Elmo firmly. "I have a plan!" Then she gathered up many large bolts of cloth and handed them to Elmo. Next she reached for her sewing basket and scissors.

"How is all this cloth and thread going to stop that terrible giant?" Elmo asked with a tearful sniff.

"You'll see," Minnie replied. "Follow me!" And she led the way to Elmo's big house. Elmo's house was the biggest house in town.

"Oh, no, Minnie," Elmo groaned. "My house is the first place he is going to look. What are we doing here?"

"Elmo," Minnie asked, "do you think you can build a cradle large enough to hold you?"

"I guess so," answered Elmo.

"Good—then go build the largest one you can. In the meantime, I'm going to sew a special giant-sized bonnet."

"But, Minnie," said Elmo, "I don't understand."

"There's no time to explain," Minnie said. "Do exactly as I say, and I promise we'll be safe from the giant. Okay?"

"Okay," agreed Elmo. Then the two set to work. Minnie made an enormous baby bonnet. And Elmo made the hugest cradle he could build.

Minnie tied the big baby bonnet under Elmo's chin and told him to put the cradle in his bedroom. "Now just hop in," Minnie told him. "Stay here with your eyes closed tight, and don't make a peep— even if that other giant comes in."

So Elmo closed his eyes and held on to the covers for dear life.

Quick as a wink, Minnie settled herself on the front porch, and she began to sew.

Pretty soon the ground began to quiver and shake. The rumbling noise came closer and closer. All the while, Minnie kept sewing. She didn't look up for so much as a second to find out what all the noise was about.

At last the shaking stopped. Minnie looked up, and up . . . and up!

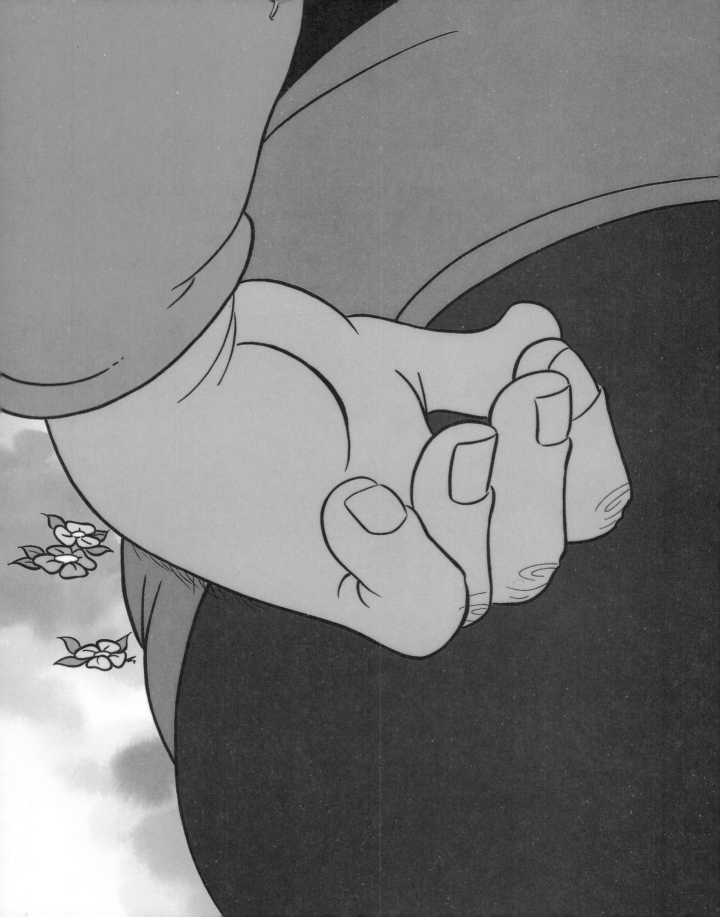

Minnie greeted the giant with a cheerful, "Can I help you?"

"I am Igor—and I have come to fight with Elmo."

"Was he expecting you?" Minnie asked.

"Of course he was expecting me!" Igor thundered. "I don't waste my time with folks as small as you! Where is Elmo?"

"Well, I only asked if Elmo was expecting you because he is out on giant business at the moment," said Minnie. "He's fighting a dragon, I believe. And I have no idea when he'll be back.

"Dear, dear—this is a problem," she added. "Would you care to come back some other time?"

"There is no other time!" Igor roared.

"Then perhaps you would care to wait instead?" Minnie suggested.

"I'll just do that," sneered Igor. "And if I find out that coward Elmo is hiding from me ..." Before he could finish, Minnie interrupted.

"I assure you, sir, that Elmo is no coward. He wouldn't think of hiding from someone your size—I mean, from someone like you," Minnie told him.

"We'll see about that," replied Igor. "I'll just wait right here until he comes back."

"Suit yourself," answered Minnie. Then she continued with her sewing.

Minnie got up and walked to Elmo's front yard.
She laid out the very long pieces of cloth she was
sewing.

"What are you sewing?" Igor demanded.

"It's a suit for Elmo, of course," Minnie replied.

Igor eyed the suit. He thought, "Why, this is the longest suit I've ever seen. It would fit a giant ten times taller than I. But no matter. I'll wait for Elmo just the same."

Igor yawned and was about to stretch out for a nice long nap when he heard something that sounded like "Achooooo" come from inside the house.

"What was that?" he roared.

"What was what?" asked Minnie. She pretended she hadn't heard the sneeze.

"That sneeze!" shouted Igor. He jumped up and looked around.

"I knew it!" he sneered. "It's just as I thought. That coward Elmo is hiding in the house. I demand to see him at once!"

"I don't know what you mean," Minnie answered. "But if you'd like to come in and look around, you're certainly welcome to do so."

Angrily, Igor searched the gigantic living room. Throwing over enormous pieces of furniture, he looked for Elmo everywhere. But, thanks to Minnie, Elmo was nowhere to be found.

"Where are the other rooms in this house?" Igor grumbled.

"Oh, did you want to see the bedroom, too?" Minnie asked. "Right this way," she said.

"By the way," Minnie added in a whisper, "the giant's baby son has a very bad cold. He's sleeping in his cradle in the back. Be sure you don't wake him up."

"Ah-ha!" cried Igor as he ran into the bedroom. There, before him, was Elmo, all wrapped up with his eyes shut tight—sleeping just like a little baby!

Igor's eyes grew wide with fear. His hands began to tremble. Large drops of sweat began to pour down his face.

"Is this the giant's baby son?" he gulped.

"Isn't that what I've been saying?" Minnie replied, busying herself about the room. She tucked in the blanket here and patted down the cover there. "Imagine—he's only six months old! Why, when he grows up, he'll look just like his father," she added proudly.

"My goodness," Igor thought to himself. "This is the biggest baby I've ever seen. If this is the size of the baby ... then the father must be huge!" He began to back slowly out of the house.

"Is something wrong?" Minnie asked.

"Nothing, nothing at all," mumbled the terrible giant as he turned to run out of the house. "By the way," he called, "don't bother telling Elmo about my visit. I'm sure he's much too busy to see me anyway." Then Igor ran away as fast as he could.

Minnie watched the not-so-terrible giant disappear from sight. Just then the giant "baby" peered out through the window.

"Well, that's the end of him," Minnie declared.

"Do you think he's gone for good?" Elmo asked.

"Oh, my, yes! I'm quite sure," Minnie said. Elmo sighed with relief. Minnie turned to gather up her things and go.

"You know, Minnie, I never would have thought that someone as small as you could protect *me* from a great big giant!" said Elmo.

"The secret," Minnie replied, "is to always keep your wits about you. Just because someone is very, very big doesn't mean he is very, very clever."

From that day on, Igor was never heard from again. And Elmo and Minnie lived happily ever after.

Think About It

Reading Faces

You can often tell how characters feel by "reading" their faces. Look at each picture below. Match each character to the word that best describes how each one feels. What happened in the story to make each character feel this way?

happy   scared   thoughtful

After your child does the activities in this book, refer to the *Young Readers Guide* for the answers to these activities and for additional games, activities, and ideas.

What's Wrong
With This Picture?

Point to the four things in this picture that aren't
quite right.

Fun With Words

Matching Sizes

Who is the *smallest?*
Who is *larger* than Minnie?

Who is *smaller* than Elmo?
Who is the *largest* of all?

Point to the things that belong to each character.

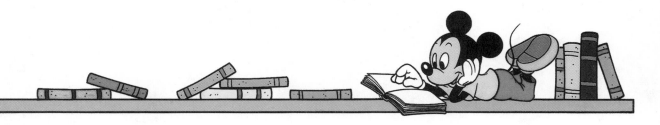

A-Maze-in' Minnie

Help Minnie find her way to Elmo's house. With your finger, trace the correct path so that Minnie can gather up all the things she needs to make a suit for Elmo.

ickey's
ickey's Young Readers Library • Mickey's Young Readers Library • Mickey's Yo
oung Readers Library • Mickey's Young Readers Library • Mickey's Young Read
ickey's Young Readers Library • Micke